To ARIANA

With all our love

from GREAT GRANNY KATH

& GREAT GRANDAD GRAHAM

from AUSTRALIA

May 2018

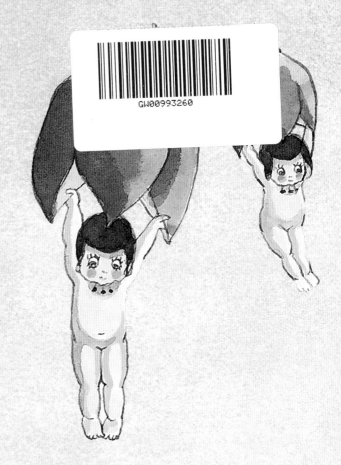

Scholastic Australia Pty Limited
PO Box 579 Gosford NSW 2250
ABN 11 000 614 577
www.scholastic.com.au

Part of the Scholastic Group
Sydney • Auckland • New York • Toronto • London • Mexico City
• New Delhi • Hong Kong • Buenos Aires • Puerto Rico

First published by Scholastic Australia in 2016.
This edition published in 2017.
Copyright © in original May Gibbs' illustrations, The Northcott Society and Cerebral Palsy Alliance 2016.
Copyright © in May Gibbs' text, The Northcott Society and Cerebral Palsy Alliance 2016.
Stories written by Jane Massam.
Illustrations inspired by May Gibbs' original illustrations.
Illustrations created by Caroline Keys.

National Library of Australia Cataloguing-in-Publication entry
Creator: Gibbs, May, 1877-1969, author.
Title: May Gibbs' tales from the gum tree / May Gibbs, Jane Massam; illustrated by Caroline Keys.
ISBN: 9781742767581(hardback)
Target Audience: For pre-school age.
Subjects: Snugglepot (Fictitious character)--Juvenile fiction.
          Cuddlepie (Fictitious character)--Juvenile fiction.
          Animals--Australia--Juvenile fiction.
          Country life--Australia--Juvenile fiction.
Other Creators/Contributors: Massam, Jane, author.
          Keys, Caroline, illustrator.
Dewey Number: A823.2

Typeset in Adobe Caslon.

Printed in China by RR Donnelley.
Scholastic Australia's policy, in association with RR Donnelley, is to use papers that are renewable and made efficiently from wood grown in responsibly managed forests, so as to minimise its environmental footprint.

Part of the proceeds help to assist the work of Cerebral Palsy Alliance of New South Wales, 321 Mona Vale Road, Terrey Hills, NSW 2084, www.cerebralpalsy.org.au and The Northcott Society, 1 Fennell Street, North Parramatta, NSW 2151, www.northcott.com.au

10 9 8 7 6 5 4 3 2 1   17 18 19 20 21 / 1

May Gibbs Tales From The Gum Tree

Gumnut Babies

A Scholastic Australia book

The Dragonfly Races

One morning, Snugglepot and Cuddlepie were lazing in the sunshine when *zoom*, a cluster of glittering dragonflies flew overhead.

'How I'd love to fly,' said Snugglepot dreamily. 'I wonder how it would feel to race through the blue, blue sky. Perhaps I might get the chance today at the Dragonfly Races!'

'I would rather stay safely on the ground,' Cuddlepie said. 'Besides, only expert fliers can ride dragonflies,' he added.

But Snugglepot pretended not to hear.

The usually sleepy bush was now bustling. Crowds of bush folk had come from far and wide to enjoy the fun, and the nuts had never seen so many of them in one place.

'Hello, young friends!' Mr Lizard called out. He was dressed so smartly, Snugglepot and Cuddlepie hardly recognised him. 'What would you like to do first?' he asked.

'I would like to ride a dragonfly!' said Snugglepot.

'I think you had better leave that to the racers,' Mr Lizard laughed. 'How about the slides?'

They had a wonderful time whizzing down the slides on their leaves, slurping cups of nectar and riding on the swings. They enjoyed themselves so much, Snugglepot forgot all about flying.

Mr Lizard called them over. 'Come and see this!'

High up in the branches above, the Boronia Babies were putting on a daring acrobatic show. The audience was spellbound as the performers swung on trapezes and somersaulted through the air.

'I hope they don't fall!' Cuddlepie whispered.

'The spiders have woven a net, so they'll be quite safe,' reassured Mr Lizard.

'Look out!' Snugglepot cried.

The audience gasped as a Boronia Baby suddenly let go of the trapeze. Using her petals as a parachute, she floated across the clearing. All the Boronia Babies were now flying through the air, laughing as the breeze filled their petals.

'It seems everyone can fly except for me!' said Snugglepot, trying not to be sad. 'I would *so* love to fly.'

'Never mind,' Mr Lizard comforted. 'Maybe when you are older, you will. To fly takes a great deal of practice.'

Snugglepot knew Mr Lizard was right. 'But I wish I was up there,' he said wistfully, watching the gliding acrobats.

Just then, there was a rustle overhead. A beautiful butterfly emerged from her cocoon, ruffling her wings to dry them in the sun. Suddenly there was another flash of colour, then another. The butterflies were waking up after their long slumber.

Cuddlepie clicked his fingers with a grin. 'I know how you can fly!'

Flagging down a butterfly, Cuddlepie whispered in her ear. She nodded and fluttered over to Snugglepot.

'My name is Sunburst. Where would you like to go?' she asked Snugglepot.

Snugglepot's eyes widened in amazement. 'Really?' he asked. 'Up to the sky, please!'

He climbed up onto the butterfly's back, and with a flap of her wings, she gently took Snugglepot upwards.

'Oh my!' cried Snugglepot. 'I'm flying, I'm really *flying!*' He couldn't believe he was up in the big blue sky, and it was simply glorious.

'Wait for me!' Cuddlepie called out to Snugglepot and hopped onto a waiting butterfly. It moved so slowly and gracefully, he felt quite safe. It was as if he was travelling on a cloud.

Waving goodbye to Mr Lizard, the butterflies took the nuts right across the whole carnival. They marvelled at all the sights far below them.

'This is amazing!' shouted Snugglepot, full of glee as his butterfly looped-the-loop. Cuddlepie smiled but was glad his did not do the same.

When the butterflies finally landed, both nuts were absolutely giddy with joy.

'Did you enjoy flying, Snugglepot?' asked Mr Lizard, who was waiting for them.

'Oh yes!' said Snugglepot, bouncing with excitement. 'Did you see me fly? I had the best time *ever!*'

'And what about you, young Cuddlepie?' Mr Lizard smiled.

'Why, flying isn't so scary after all!' Cuddlepie said. 'Next time, shall we find a dragonfly?'

Snugglepot to the Rescue

'Let's go, Cuddlepie!' said Snugglepot, dancing with excitement. 'It's time for our lesson!'

'Do you really think we'll be able to paddle our own boats?' asked Cuddlepie.

'As sure as nuts have caps!' said Snugglepot, pulling on his friend's hand.

The Wattle Babies had promised to show Snugglepot and Cuddlepie how to paddle across the creek. Wattle Babies are very good teachers, as they are always so cheerful and encouraging.

It was a warm spring afternoon, and the nuts were glad when they reached the cool creek, lined with shady peppermint gums.

'There they are!' Snugglepot pointed at the brightly-coloured Wattle Babies down at the creek bank. The friendly frogs were helping them with the boats.

'Hello, Bright Eyes!' Snugglepot and Cuddlepie called out when they saw their gumnut friend waiting for them.

'Are you ready to set sail?' asked Bright Eyes after their lesson.

'Um, I suppose so,' said Cuddlepie with a frown. 'The boats look awfully *small.*'

Bright Eyes laughed. 'Don't worry, Cuddlepie! These canoes are made from the finest seed pods. They are perfectly watertight!'

Just then, some of the Wattle and Boronia children began climbing onto swings. Spun from the strongest spider-silk, they hung from the low-lying branches of the river gums. The children swung out far over the creek, letting go to plunge into the rippling water below.

Splash! It was a wonderful game that had them shrieking with laughter.

'Just remember not to stand up in your boat!' Bright Eyes called out as Snugglepot and Cuddlepie settled into their canoes.

The nuts followed Bright Eyes out across the creek.

'Wait for me!' Cuddlepie shouted as he went round in a circle.

'You need to paddle on both sides,' called Bright Eyes, laughing. 'Watch me!'

Once he got the hang of paddling, Cuddlepie started to enjoy bobbing across the water.

Snugglepot was also enjoying gliding across the water. 'This is the life!'

There was a commotion as a paddleboat went by, churning up the water. A family of lizards was pedalling the large wheel with their long, strong legs.

'Look, it's Mr Lizard!' said Cuddlepie. 'Hello, Mr and Mrs Lizard!' he waved.

But the lizards were too busy laughing to notice the little gumnut. Cuddlepie stood up to attract their attention.

'Mr Liz . . . whoa!' shouted Cuddlepie, wobbling dangerously in the wash of waves. He lost his balance and fell out of his canoe head-first, disappearing into the water with a gentle plop.

Splish! Splash! Splosh! The Boronia and Wattle Babies continued with their noisy game and the paddleboat swished around the bend . . . there was so much going on, the lifeguards didn't notice Cuddlepie had fallen into the creek.

Luckily, someone else *had* noticed.

Reaching the other bank, Snugglepot was now clutching one of the spider-web swings.

'Hold on, Cuddlepie!' Snugglepot shouted to his friend as he jumped.

Swoosh! Snugglepot swooped across the water, reaching down and stretching out his hand.

'Got you!' he cried, pulling a very wet gumnut out of the creek.

'I'm soaked from my head to my toes!' Cuddlepie spluttered, sailing through the air.

Everyone gasped as Snugglepot gently dropped him onto dry land.

'I d-d-don't th-th-think boating is for me!' Cuddlepie shivered as Snugglepot wrapped him in a warm leaf. The air grew chilly as the sun began to set, so Bright Eyes built a crackling campfire. 'You'll be dry and toasty in no time,' he told his wet friend.

The group joined Cuddlepie around the warm fire and roasted some delicious seeds for their supper. Cuddlepie was beginning to feel a bit better now he had some yummy honey tea inside him.

Everyone was talking about Snugglepot's daring rescue of Cuddlepie.

'The way you came flying through the air was simply rippling!' said a young frog admiringly.

'You got there so quickly! It was treetop!' said a Boronia Baby.

Bright Eyes laughed. 'What an adventure you have had. I didn't expect anyone to do any fishing today!'

'I think *I* landed the catch of the day!' said Snugglepot, hugging his friend and smiling.

Everyone roared with laughter, Cuddlepie loudest of all.

The Moonlight Pageant

It was a few days until Mrs Kookaburra's birthday party. Snugglepot and Cuddlepie were very excited.

'Let's take a trip to the Big City to buy her a special present,' said Snugglepot.

'Oh, yes!' cried Cuddlepie, clapping his hands. 'I'm sure we'll find a very special present there!'

So the nuts emptied their piggy banks and put their money inside their hats. The Big City was very far away so they took cricket taxis.

Snugglepot and Cuddlepie enjoyed the ride, but they were glad when the sky turned pink and they could stop for the night. 'I'm so tired!' yawned Cuddlepie.

'Look, butterfly cocoons!' Snugglepot pointed to a nearby branch. 'Let's borrow two,' he said. Wrapped up in the soft silk, the nuts were soon asleep.

But in the middle of the night, they were suddenly awoken by a loud howling beneath their tree.

'Wh-wh-what is that?' Cuddlepie trembled, peeping out of his cocoon.

'I do-do-don't know,' Snugglepot said with his hands over his ears.

'There they go again! Makin' such a din!' an elderly blossom complained, looking out from her tiny house above. 'Nobody can get any sleep around here!'

Looking down, Snugglepot and Cuddlepie saw two koalas bathed in moonlight, howling with happiness. And lots of tired little nut and blossom faces peeking out all around.

'What are they doing?' Snugglepot asked the old lady.

'Singin'! Mr and Mrs Koala always do it when the moon is out. Doesn't much sound like singing to me!' The blossom went inside, grumbling to herself.

'Excuse me, Mr and Mrs Koala!' Snugglepot called out. 'Could you please be quieter? We are all trying to sleep!'

Mr Koala laughed. 'Ho ho, young nut. Isn't the moon beautiful? We love it s-o-o-o-o . . .' and the awful noise continued.

'We need to make the koalas forget about singing to the moon,' Cuddlepie said. 'Then everyone can get a good night's sleep. I have an idea!'

They gathered the weary neighbours and told them of their plan. Nodding and smiling, everyone went back to their beds as the moon slid behind the clouds.

The next day, everyone eagerly came together—they were going to put on a magnificent show! They sewed feathers, petals and leaves, and Snugglepot and Cuddlepie spent all day helping the performers practise. They were so hard at work, they forgot all about their journey to the Big City.

'Don't worry, Cuddlepie, now *I* have an idea!' said Snugglepot. He scribbled a note and gave it to a cricket to deliver.

When it became dark and the moon once more lit up the night sky, Mr and Mrs Koala climbed down from their tree. Before they could open their mouths to sing, Snugglepot spoke.

'Mr and Mrs Koala, just for you, we would like to present the Moonlight Pageant!' he said, bowing grandly.

One by one, the performers came onto the stage. The Flannel Flower Babies performed an elegant ballet, accompanied by the Frog and Cricket Choir.

Then the Wattle Babies put on a funny magic show. They can hide a lot of things in their fluffy yellow clothes, you know!

'By gum, I haven't laughed so much in years!' said Mr Koala as another act appeared.

Mrs and Mrs Koala were so enchanted, they didn't look up at the moon once.

When the curtain finally fell, the clapping and cheering was deafening.

The night was a huge success!

'Well, well, here are my good friends!' a familiar voice said.

'Mrs Kookaburra! What are you doing here?' asked Cuddlepie.

Mrs Kookaburra held out a note. 'I heard about your show.
So I had to fly over and see it for myself. And what a treat it was!'
she smiled. 'It's a *wonderful* birthday present!'

Snugglepot and Cuddlepie grinned back. 'Happy birthday,
Mrs Kookaburra!'